Thanks to
Sophie Jaulmes
— ED

Published in English in Canada and the USA in 2021 by
Groundwood Books
First published in French in 2020 as *Sans orage ni nuage* by Albin
Michel Jeunesse
Copyright © Albin Michel Jeunesse, 2020
English translation copyright © 2021 by Groundwood Books

Groundwood Books / House of Anansi Press
groundwoodbooks.com

Groundwood Books respectfully acknowledges that the land on
which we operate is the Traditional Territory of many Nations,
including the Anishinabeg, the Wendat and the Haudenosaunee.
It is also the Treaty Lands of the Mississaugas of the Credit.

We gratefully acknowledge the Government of
Canada for their financial support of our publishing
program.

With the participation of the Government of Canada
Avec la participation du gouvernement du Canada | Canadä

Library and Archives Canada Cataloguing in Publication
Title: The day the rain moved in / Éléonore Douspis ; translated by
Shelley Tanaka.
Other titles: Sans orage ni nuage. English
Names: Douspis, Éléonore, author, illustrator. | Tanaka, Shelley,
translator.
Description: Translation of: Sans orage ni nuage.
Identifiers: Canadiana (print) 20200267728 | Canadiana
(ebook) 20200267760 | ISBN 9781773064819 (hardcover) | ISBN
9781773064826 (EPUB) | ISBN 9781773064833 (Kindle)
Subjects: LCGFT: Picture books.
Classification: LCC PZ7.1.D38 Da 2021 | DDC j843/.92—dc23

The art was created digitally.
Printed and bound in China

FSC
www.fsc.org
MIX
Paper from
responsible sources
FSC® C008047

THE DAY THE RAIN MOVED IN

Éléonore Douspis

TRANSLATED BY SHELLEY TANAKA

Groundwood Books
House of Anansi Press
Toronto / Berkeley

It's raining this morning. It rained yesterday, too.
Pauline and Louis watch as the raindrops hit the floor again and again.
No one feels like playing when it's this wet.

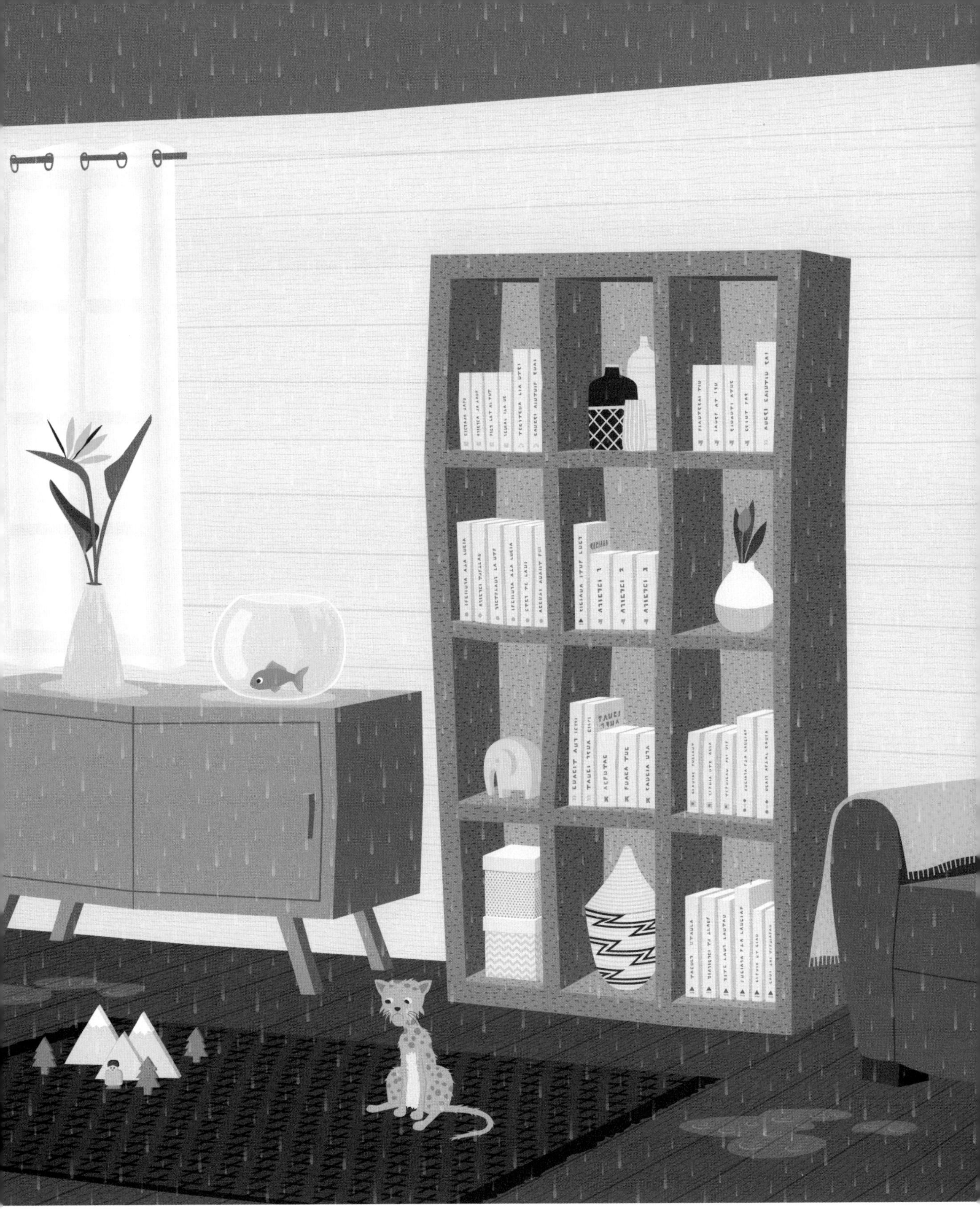

It's raining in every room in the house.
There's a puddle in the living room that grows a bit bigger each day.

There's been no storm, no clouds. The rain has simply moved into the house. No one invited it in.

The whole family searches for a leak. But they can't find a single gap, not even a tiny crack.

It's raining inside the house. And the water is pouring in from nowhere.

Outside, the sun is shining. Pauline and Louis head down the path to school.
They're wearing their raincoats. Water drips down their foreheads.

In the schoolyard, they stand off to one side.
They don't dare join in with the others, in case someone finds out about their secret.

Back at home, not much has changed. It's so damp that the walls are covered with mildew. And look! A seedling has sprouted between the floor tiles.

There's nothing they can do. The puddle grows into a pond.
Ferns, reeds and water lilies open up, and frogs move in.
The grumpy cat won't leave his bed.

The little seedling transforms into a tree bursting with life.
Leaves and branches snake through the house, eating up more and more space.
Pauline lets the goldfish out of its bowl.

Curious, the children from school crowd around the window of this strange house.
Pauline and Louis are surprised when their father opens the door and invites everyone in.

The children can't believe their eyes. They have never seen anything like this!
The table has become an island, the staircase a dock, the cat's bed a canoe.
Together they explore this unlikely new playground.

Suddenly, there is a cracking sound. The branches pierce through the walls and roof, reaching up to the sky ...

And then sunlight floods into the house.
Pauline and Louis take off their raincoats and break into smiles.

The rain has stopped.